Meet My Grandparents

Papa Lemon was born in West, Mississippi on Dec. 6, 1896, and passed away on Oct. 29, 1973. The last time I saw my grandfather was when they closed the coffin at his funeral.I could not believe that would be the end. No more games of checkers or taking me to Miss Annie B's General Store for candy or pop. Ten years was not enough, but I thank God for giving me the vision to share my grandfather with the world. Kids of all ages, I give you my grandfather, Papa Lemon.

Mama Sarah and Papa Lemon

Mama Sarah, the wife of Papa Lemon, was born in West, Mississippi on Jan. 26, 1903. My grandmother lived to be 101 years old. She was the sweetest lady I ever knew. I never heard my grandmother raise her voice. I loved for her to tell me stories about how she grew up, and the life she had with Papa Lemon. She found good in everyone, never seeing the negative in people. With her last words she looked to heaven and said "It's so beautiful," and passed away, and that's how she was so beautiful.

Papa Lemon and Mama Sarah had nine children and numerous grand and great grand children.

Illustrations by Joshua Wallace.

Printed in the United States of America.
Lehman Riley/Matter of Africa America Time Corporation®
P.O. Box 11535
Minneapolis, MN 55411
Library of Congress Catalog Card No. 2006926302
ISBN 0-9760523-2-6

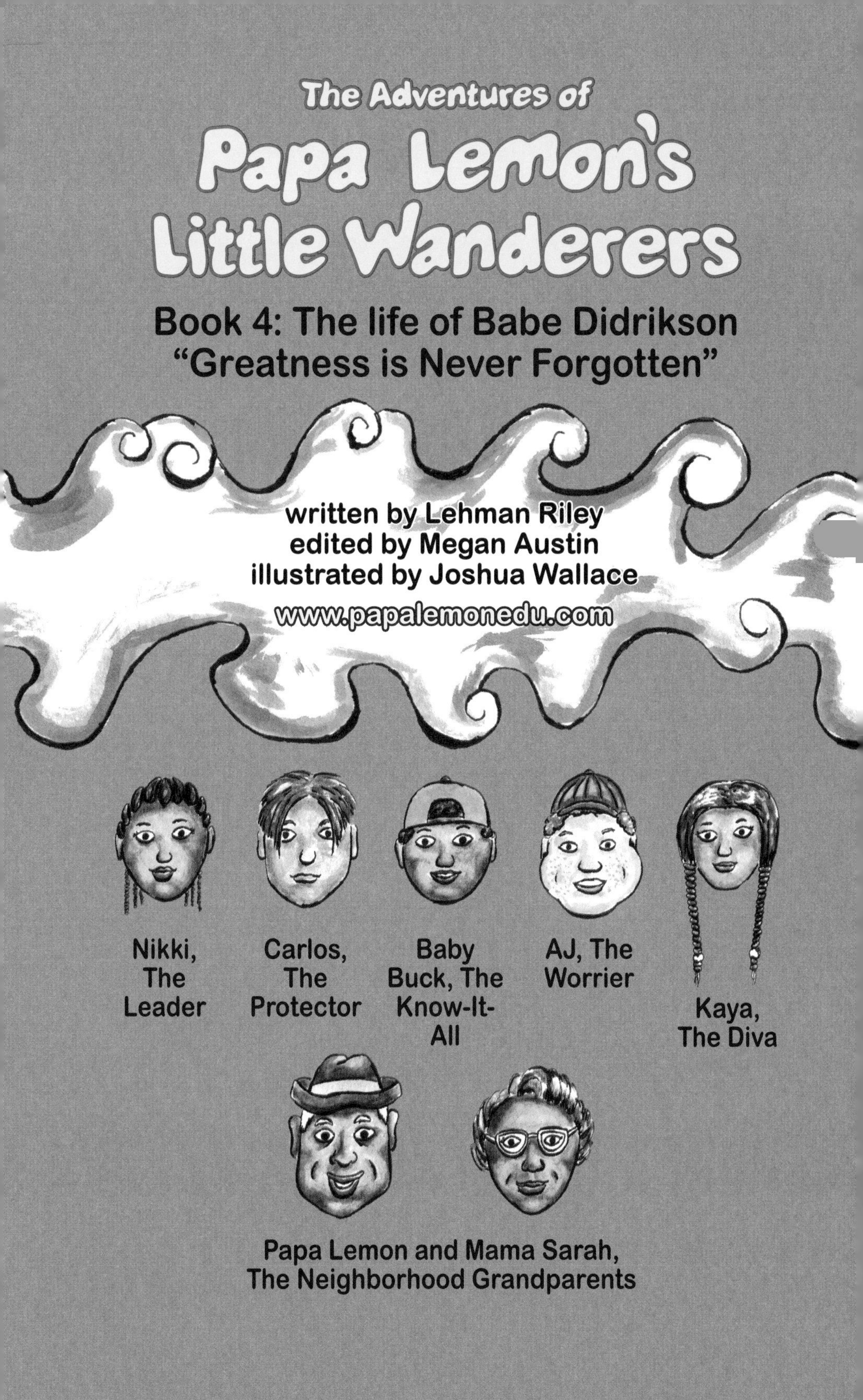
The Adventures of
Papa Lemon's
Little Wanderers
Book 4: The life of Babe Didrikson
"Greatness is Never Forgotten"
written by Lehman Riley
edited by Megan Austin
illustrated by Joshua Wallace
www.papalemonedu.com
Nikki, The Leader
Carlos, The Protector
Baby Buck, The Know-It-All
AJ, The Worrier
Kaya, The Diva
Papa Lemon and Mama Sarah, The Neighborhood Grandparents

"That's the end of our story, The Kings Of Baseball. After recess I want each of you to write about one of the great sluggers you learned about," said Mrs. Gonzalez. The bell rang and the kids ran out to the playground with baseball bats and gloves. They were going to finish playing the fifth grade championship game against another class. Carlos led the group and Baby Buck began to chant, "We're number one! We're number one!"

Nikki, Kaya and AJ started to warm up, throwing the ball to each other and swinging the bat as they watched the other class practice. Carlos gathered his team around him and told them his plan. "Ok the score is seven to ten and we are down by three runs. We have the last turn at bat. I will bat first. AJ, you're second. Kaya, you're third. Baby Buck is fourth. Nikki, you're after him and Ginger, you're after Nikki," said Carlos, pointing to each player.

As Carlos gave his instructions, the other team began to shout. “Let’s play! You’re stalling because you know you’re going to lose,” they called. Carlos grabbed a bat and gave a wink to his teammates as he stepped up to the plate.

“Show me your best pitch, Ronnie,” Carlos said with a grin. His words wiped the smile off the pitcher’s face. He wound up and threw his best. Carlos kept his eyes on the ball and gave a mighty swing. CRACK!

Baby Buck jumped up screaming, “IT’S A HOME RUN!” Everyone watched in awe as Carlos rounded third base. All his teammates gave him high fives as he crossed home plate. “You’re up next, AJ,” Baby Buck said.

AJ walked up to the plate and waited for the pitch. Ronnie knew that AJ was the best hitter on the team. “There is no way I’m throwing you a strike,” he muttered as he threw his pitch. Ball one. Ball two. Ball three. Ball four. AJ ran to first base. Their secret weapon was next.

Everyone in school knew that Ronnie liked Kaya. She used that fact to her team's advantage, smiling and waving to Ronnie as she walked up to the plate. He turned red and smiled back at her. "Ronnie, don't throw the ball too hard, okay? It hurts my hand when I hit it." Her teammates laughed. They knew Ronnie would let her get to first base.

"Don't worry, I won't hit you," Ronnie said and he tossed the ball nice and slow. Kaya swung and hit it over his head. She ran to first base, sending AJ to second.

Baby Buck ran to the plate. "You guys had better back up because this is going to be the game-winning hit. I'm sending this one over the fence!" he proclaimed, as he gestured toward the fence with the bat.

"Back up," Ronnie said to his teammates. He threw the pitch and, to everyone's surprise, Baby Buck bunted the

ball and ran to first base. "I can't believe you fell for that," Baby Buck laughed, "come on Nikki, bring us home!"

Then Nikki walked up to the plate. "You don't have to worry about the ball hurting my hands," she told Ronnie as she took a practice swing.

Ronnie's teammates shouted, "Strike her out so everyone will know that we are the champions of the fifth grade!" Ronnie wound up his pitch. "You asked for this, Nikki," he said and threw a fastball. Nikki took a swing and missed. Strike one.

Nikki stepped back. "Not bad, Ronnie. Let me see one more just like that." Ronnie narrowed his eyes and tried his best imitation of the big league baseball players. He had a piece of bubble gum in his mouth and he stared at Nikki as he spit. Nikki swiped her braids from her eyes and gripped the bat tightly. Ronnie was more determined to strike her out and threw the ball harder than before. Nikki gave a swing that would make Hank Aaron proud and connected with the ball, sending it sailing out of the schoolyard and over the fence!

Ronnie threw down his glove. "That was a lucky hit!" he shouted.

"Lucky hit or not, we're the champs!" Baby Buck yelled back. Nikki reached home plate and Carlos and AJ picked her up on their shoulders. "Now that was a home run like Babe Ruth would have hit!" Carlos said with a grin.

Nikki answered, "No, I think it was more like a Babe Didrikson home run."

The team carried Nikki into the school. "Babe who?" Baby Buck asked, but no one could hear him over all the commotion. "We're number one!" they chanted through the hallways and all the way into the classroom.

Mrs. Gonzalez watched the celebration. "What a game! You showed great teamwork

MATH QUIZ TOMORROW
Kirby Puckett Carries the Twins Through 1991 World Series
Twins
34

out there. I'm so proud to have you kids in my class. You looked like the Minnesota Twins when they beat the Atlanta Braves in 1991. Nikki, you were just like Kirby Puckett when he hit the winning home run in the last inning," she said proudly.

"Thanks Mrs. Gonzalez, but I prefer Babe Didrikson," said Nikki.

"There you go again! Who is this Didrikson person that you keep talking about?" Baby Buck asked with a puzzled look.

"She was one of America's greatest athletes," explained Nikki. "Isn't that right, Mrs. Gonzalez?"

"You're right, Nikki. She was one of our bright stars in the 1930's. She excelled in many sports, baseball was just one of them. Babe Didrikson won Olympic gold medals in several events in 1932, and she was one of the best golfers ever to play the game. I think it would be a great idea for you kids to research Babe Didrikson for extra credit this weekend," said Mrs. Gonzalez.

The class groaned. "Thanks a lot, Nikki!" Just then, the bell rang and class was dismissed.

As the Little Wanderers started to walk home, they heard a car honk behind them. To their surprise, it was Papa Lemon and Mama Sarah. The car pulled over to the curb and Mama Sarah rolled down the window. The kids were full of energy from their baseball game and Baby Buck could be heard talking above all the others, telling the grandparents about Nikki's heroic play.

Papa Lemon interrupted the group with a chuckle, "I know, I know! We were there! Oh, and by the way, Nikki, I think this belongs to you." Papa Lemon handed her the ball she had hit out of the schoolyard.

"Thank you," Nikki said with a smile.

"You know Nikki, you really reminded me of Babe Didrikson when you hit that ball," said Mama Sarah.

"Please tell us what you know about Babe Didrikson! Nikki has been talking about her ever since we finished the game," pleaded Baby Buck.

"Well, I can tell you that Babe Didrikson was one of the world's greatest athletes in the 1930's. In fact, she was one of the greatest all-around athletes I've ever seen. She played basketball, baseball, golf and tennis. She ran track, she bowled and she was a boxer."

"Boxing?" Baby Buck interrupted.

"Yes, that's right! She could scrap with some of the roughest kids in the neighborhood," Papa Lemon replied. "She was very fast. Maybe that's how she was able to hit baseballs so far. I could tell you stories, but there's a better way for you to learn about her," he said, raising his eyebrows.

"Yeah! We don't need a story—let's go

meet her," Carlos proposed.

"Why don't you go back to 1925 and watch Babe in action?" suggested Papa Lemon. "I think you will enjoy what you will see."

"What will we see?" Nikki begged. Mama Sarah laughed and told the kids to climb into the car for a ride to their adventure.

The Little Wanderers' curiosity was running wild by the time they pulled up to Papa Lemon's house. They burst out of the car, tore through the house and ran up to the attic as quickly as they could. They flung open the old trunk to look for clothes for their adventure. "What did they wear back then?" AJ asked.

"Whatever it was, I'll make it look good," Kaya answered, holding up a dress.

"Oh! I found what we could wear! Look! Uniforms!" Carlos shouted.

"They feel like sacks. I can't play

baseball wearing this, I'll be scratching too much," said Kaya.

"The way you play, it won't matter," Baby Buck joked.

Nikki was a step ahead of everyone and had already put on her outfit. "I'm ready! How do I look?" she said, with her arms open wide to show off the uniform.

"You look great, just like a baseball player from the old days," said Mama Sarah from the doorway. "Now finish getting ready and get to your adventure."

The kids got dressed and ran to the shed where Papa Lemon was waiting for them. He was cleaning the train, one of the things he still enjoyed since retiring from his own adventures. "Wow! Look at you kids! You really look like a team."

"Yes, they sure do make a handsome group," said Mama Sarah from behind them. The kids turned around and were surprised to see her standing in the doorway as they

50

prepared to leave.

"You never watch us go, What are you doing here?" said Kaya.

Mama Sarah walked toward Papa Lemon and he put his arm around her. "Well, I thought I would see you kids off on this trip. I was too nervous to watch you leave for your other adventures, but I know you will have fun with this one."

"But just remember, kids—even though this adventure isn't as dangerous as some of the others, the same rules still apply," said Papa Lemon.

"Okay," said Carlos. "As long as Baby Buck doesn't run ahead and get in trouble, we'll all be okay," he said, only half joking as he gave his friend a playful nudge.

The kids climbed into the train and Nikki set the dial for 1925 as everyone waved goodbye to Papa Lemon and Mama Sarah. Kaya pulled the gearshift back and off they went!

In an instant, the train had landed in a cornfield. Baby Buck leaped off the train

and tangled himself on a scarecrow on his way to the ground. "Help! Help! Somebody get me down!" he yelled. The rest of the Little Wanderers looked at him and laughed. "Don't just stand there! Help me!" he shouted, spitting hay from his mouth.

Carlos came to Baby Buck's rescue, untangling him and lifting him down to the ground. "That's what I'm talking about, Baby Buck. Stop running ahead of us. One day that's going to get you in big trouble," he scolded with a smile.

"Let's get out of here. I feel like this cornfield is going to swallow me up," Kaya said as she climbed down from the train and looked around. "Hey, where is AJ?" The group looked around and found AJ at the back of the train eating fresh popcorn. "Where did you get that?" asked Kaya.

"Well, I pulled the husk off a piece of corn, put it in front of the engine and the heat made it pop. Try some, it's good!" AJ

said with his mouth full. The kids helped themselves.

"Not bad! It just needs a little butter," said Nikki. After a moment, she stopped chewing. "Do you hear that? It sounds like voices," she said.

"Yeah, it's coming from that direction," said Carlos, pointing through the cornfield.

The kids walked a short distance to the edge of the field and saw a group of older kids playing baseball in a meadow across a dirt road.

"Hey, do you guys want to play with us?" called a rugged, athletic girl. "We need four more people to make the teams even."

"Yeah, we'll play," said Carlos as he led the others to the field.

"I'll keep score since you only need four players," said Kaya.

"We'll only play if we can all be on the same team," AJ added.

"No big deal," said the girl as she

50
00
22

told three of her friends to join the Little Wanderers. "You guys look a little young so I'll take it easy on you. I don't want you to go home crying to your mother, telling her that the big kid played too rough. Don't get confused, though—I am playing to win. To show you how nice I am, I will let your team bat first," said the girl.

"Lay off them," said one of the older boys. "Let's just have fun."

"Don't worry about us," said Nikki. "We've played this game a few times before."

"Good, then let's play ball," said the girl.

The players gathered and Baby Buck introduced the group to their new teammates. "I'm Baby Buck and this is AJ. That's Carlos. Nikki is the girl with the braids over there and Kaya will be keeping score," he said, pointing to his friends as he named them.

"My name is Butch," said one

of the boys.

"My name is Wilbur. Just call me Will," said the other.

"I'm Lou—short for Louella," said a girl who had joined them. "Let me tell you about Mildred," said Lou with a nod toward the girl who had greeted them. "She's a great ball player and she's very competitive. She plays hard which makes us play hard too."

"Yeah and she gets angry if she loses a game," Butch informed them. "And don't call her Mildred. She hates that. I do it just to get under her skin."

"What should we call her then?" asked AJ.

"Call her Babe," said Lou.

"Babe? Are you telling me that's Babe Didrikson?" said Nikki, tugging on her braids in excitement.

"Yeah. What's the big deal?" asked Lou.

"We're from another town and we've heard she's really good," said Nikki. "How did she get the name ‘Babe’ anyway?”

“Last year we were right here playing a game with some older kids. One of the guys was teasing her and said girls shouldn’t play baseball because they could get hurt. He told her he was going to strike her out and that she should go home and bake him a pie. But Babe kept a cool head. She said, ‘Let’s see if you can throw as fast as you can talk,’” said Lou.

“Do you see that tree over there? Can you see where that branch is broken?” asked Will, pointing at a tree in the distance. “Babe broke that branch when she hit the ball that day. The kid who threw the pitch named her Babe because he said Babe Ruth was the last person he saw hit like that,” explained Will. Nikki shook her head in amazement as she looked at the tree.

“That has to be close to three hundred feet away,” she whispered to herself.

“Hey! Are you guys going to talk or

play?" called Babe from the pitcher's mound.

"I hope you are good," Lou said to the Little Wanderers as they took their positions on the field.

Lou was the first at bat. "Easy out," Babe called. Lou swung and missed three times and went to sit on the bench with the others. Babe was pitching well.

Butch looked at the Little Wanderers. "Can you guys hit?"

"Let me show you," said AJ, grabbing a bat and taking his place at the plate. Babe's first pitch blew right by him. AJ stepped back and looked at his team. "Not bad!" He dug his feet into the dirt and got ready for the next pitch.

CRACK! AJ connected with Babe's second pitch and sent the ball sailing into the outfield. He ran the bases as his team cheered him on. Babe could not believe what had just happened. "No more easy pitches," she said.

Butch was next up to bat. "Okay Mildred, I'm ready for you," he said, egging her on.

Babe shot him a look and threw a wicked curve ball that spun Butch around like a top. He picked himself up off the ground and dusted off his pants. "Where did that come from?" he asked.

"Call me Mildred again and you'll see one better than that," Babe responded. Her team laughed.

Nikki was watching the game with wide eyes. "I can't believe I'm going to have a chance to hit one of Babe Didrikson's pitches," she whispered to Kaya. As they talked, the girls heard Butch strike out a second time.

"Get ready because you're up next," said Kaya. "Pretend you're at school and Ronnie is the one pitching."

"There's no way I can pretend that's Ronnie!" said Nikki, watching Babe hurl a third ball at Butch. Strike three.

Butch came back to the bench. "I think I made her mad. Who's next?"

"This is your chance. Show her what you've got," Carlos said, handing a bat to Nikki. She took a deep breath.

"Come on, Nikki! We need a hit!" cheered Baby Buck. Nikki swung the bat as she walked toward the plate.

"Oh, it looks like I have a hitter here," Babe called, working the ball into her glove.

Nikki was so nervous she could barely stand, let alone hit a ball thrown by Babe Didrikson. Babe wound up her pitch and released.

Swoosh! The pitch was followed by laughter from the other team as the ball whizzed by Nikki, knocking her to the ground. She couldn't believe how fast Babe could throw.

"It's okay, Nikki," called Kaya. "You can do it!"

Nikki got up and ran one hand over

her braids, bit down on her bottom lip and waited for the next pitch. Babe smirked and threw the ball.

Nikki's eyes followed the baseball as it came closer. At the last moment, she stepped toward it and took a solid swing, hitting a line drive right toward the pitcher's mound. Nikki watched in horror as the ball hit Babe and she fell to the ground like a ton of bricks. She didn't move to get up.

"Oh no! I killed Babe Didrikson!" Nikki sobbed. Both teams ran to the mound. Nikki leaned over Babe and apologized repeatedly, as the tears fell from her eyes. "I'm so sorry. You have to be okay," she cried. "There's so much more you have to do. You're going to be a great athlete. You're going to be an American hero. You are the reason I love to play baseball," she said though her tears.

Babe's eyes flickered and opened as she raised a hand to feel the bump on her forehead. She looked at Nikki. "You can play

on my team any day," she said with a grin. Everyone laughed with relief.

Carlos and Butch helped Babe back to her feet. "Maybe we should call it a day," Kaya suggested.

"Yeah, we need to get Babe home and get some ice on that bump," said Will.

"Do you guys want to play with us next week?" Lou asked.

"We won't be in town, but thanks for asking," Baby Buck said.

The two groups parted ways and the Little Wanderers walked back through the cornfield toward the train. Kaya put her arm around Nikki. "Don't take it too hard," she said. "Accidents happen."

The kids climbed into the train. AJ set the dial and pulled the gearshift to take them home. In an instant, they were back in Papa Lemon's shed. The friends found him drinking lemonade on the porch while Mama Sarah watered her flowers. "How was

00
22
3
50

your visit?" Papa Lemon asked.

"It was okay," Nikki said, looking at the ground.

"Just okay?" Mama Sarah inquired.

"Well, Nikki almost killed Babe Didrikson," Baby Buck explained.

"What?!" said Mama Sarah.

"Nikki hit a line drive that smacked Babe in the head and knocked her out," Baby Buck explained, punching his hand for emphasis.

"Oh my goodness!" Mama Sarah exclaimed.

"She said she was alright and she told me I could play on her team any day," Nikki said, brightening as she spoke.

"Let's go up to the attic and write our extra credit report while this is all still fresh in our minds," Kaya said.

The Little Wanderers sat down around the large trunk and tried to think of what to write about Babe Didrikson. Mama Sarah had supplied the kids with snacks and Papa Lemon's old journal to get them started. "Well, we know her real name was Mildred," Carlos said.

"And we know she went to the Olympics and set a world record in 1932," Kaya added. She thumbed through Papa Lemon's journal looking for more facts to add. "It says here that she was born in Port Arthur, Texas and that her parents were from Norway," she said.

Nikki got up and started pacing back and forth. "What's wrong, Nikki?" AJ asked.

"I just can't stop thinking about what happened at that baseball game," she said. "There's no way we went back in time just to see me knock Babe Didrikson out."

"Yeah. Seeing her play that one game made me really want to learn more about her," Kaya said.

"She did so much in her lifetime! We have to go back and get a better idea of what she accomplished. Are you guys with me?" Nikki said.

The kids nodded. "Sure, Nikki."

Nikki led the group out to the backyard where Papa Lemon and Mama Sarah were now feeding the chickens. Papa Lemon could see that Nikki was troubled. "What's on your mind?" he asked.

"Papa Lemon, we have to go back to see Babe Didrikson again," Nikki explained. "She was such an inspiring woman; I have to see how great she really was. I want to see her compete in the Olympics."

"I think that's a great idea!" said Papa Lemon. As he walked the kids back to the train, he told them about all the athletes they would see. "But none were as great as Babe."

The gang climbed into the train and Kaya set the dial for 1932. "Good bye, Papa Lemon!" the kids said for the second time that day. Kaya pulled the gearshift. SWOOSH! Away they went.

The train came to a halt behind the enormous Los Angeles Memorial Coliseum, site of the 1932 Olympics. There was a lot of commotion, so everyone who noticed the train thought it was just part of the parade. No one in the crowd was the least bit suspicious.

Everyone around them was full of laughter and excitement. "There are so many people from so many places and they're all here to see their special heroes," said Nikki as they looked around. "We'll have to make sure to stick together, so follow me," said Nikki. "That includes you, Baby Buck."

Baby Buck looked at her with doubt. "Alright," he said. Carlos pulled Baby Buck's cap down over his eyes and nudged him to follow Nikki. AJ and Kaya followed close behind to make sure he didn't get lost in the crowd.

As the Little Wanderers approached

the gate, they realized they didn't have any tickets to get into the arena. When the kids reached the man taking tickets, he shook his head. "I'm sorry. I can't let you in without tickets—you'll have to leave," he said.

"Great. Now what?" asked Baby Buck.

"I'm not giving up that easily," Nikki answered. "We'll just have to get in another way."

"Okay, we're with you," said Kaya. "What's your plan?"

"Back by the train, I saw a door behind a fence covered with plants. We can squeeze through the fence where few of the plants are missing and the door should lead us inside," Nikki explained to her friends. The group walked back to the train and saw the fence. Just as she had said, some of the plants were missing, revealing a hole that was the perfect size for a determined fifth grader to slip through.

The kids glanced around hastily. “I don’t think anyone is watching,” said Baby Buck. One by one, they went through the fence and quickly slipped past the door. They found themselves in a hallway at the back of the arena.

“Let’s go,” said Nikki as she started down the hallway.

“Hey! Come back here!” shouted an angry voice. The Little Wanderers spun around and saw a large man in a uniform coming after them.

“It’s the guard! Go!” shouted Baby Buck. The kids took off, running toward a large group of people ahead of them. The

overweight guard couldn't keep up and leaned against a wall to catch his breath as the children escaped into the crowd.

Carlos wiped the sweat off his face with the front of his shirt. "Whew! That was a close call. We'd better find a safe spot to watch the events before that guard comes to find us," he said.

AJ spotted the perfect hiding place. Underneath the first row of bleachers, there were some boxes, equipment and just enough room for five kids. They were well hidden and had a perfect view of the events!

"Look, Nikki—there's Babe!" Kaya said, grabbing Nikki's arm. She pointed to the side of the field where Babe Didrikson was lining up for the 80-meter hurdles.

The crowd grew quiet as the

announcer called for the athletes to take their marks. After a long moment, a gun was fired to signal the start of the race. Babe took off like a bullet. She stayed ahead of the other women all the way to the finish line and her determination paid off. Babe finished with a time of 11.7 seconds, winning the gold medal and breaking the world record.

"Did you see her? That was unbelievable! I've never seen anyone run like that! Those other women didn't even have a chance," Nikki screamed out.

"Calm down! If you keep yelling like that, we'll get kicked out before we see any more events," Kaya said, giving Nikki's arm a squeeze.

"I know, I'll try to be quiet. It's just so exciting!"

The next event was the javelin and the announcer reminded the audience that this was the first time there had ever been an Olympic women's javelin competition. Once again, Babe was in top form. She ran and released the long javelin with a powerful throw. Everybody held their breath as they watched it sail through the air. When it came down, the crowd cheered. Babe had thrown the javelin 143 feet and 4 inches and won another gold medal.

Baby Buck's eyes were wide. "I didn't know a girl could throw like that!"

Babe's third event was the high jump and it was her toughest competition by far. Babe jumped well, tying for first place with a woman named Jane Smiley. They each broke the world record and tied for the gold medal with a height of 5 feet and 5.25 inches.

"What's going to happen?" asked AJ. "If they both jumped the same height, who wins?"

The Little Wanderers watched the field, waiting to see the results. After a few moments, the official announced the winner. "Due to a technicality, the gold medal goes to Jane Smiley and Babe Didrikson takes the silver."

"What?" shouted Baby Buck. "That's not fair! Their jumps were the same!"

"Just because Babe didn't get the gold medal, doesn't mean she wasn't just as good as the girl who did," AJ said.

As Babe was leaving the high jump area, she passed the Little Wanderers' hiding place. It was pure chance that she noticed the familiar faces among the boxes and equipment under the bleachers. She walked closer and laughed when she realized who she was looking at. "What do you know? It's the little slugger," she said, pointing to Nikki. "Have you been playing any baseball lately? Tell me you are because it would be a waste of talent if you're not."

"You were great out there," Nikki said, grinning at her hero.

"Thanks kid." Babe looked over her shoulder. "I'd better get out of here—my

coach is probably looking for me. You'd better get going too, before the guards find you," she said.

The gang of friends climbed out from underneath the bleachers and dusted themselves off. Nikki stared out at the field with a big grin on her face. "Snap out of it, we've got to go!" AJ said.

Nikki shook her head. "Yeah, you're right," she agreed.

"Are you satisfied with our adventure?" Carlos asked.

"It couldn't have been any better," Nikki answered.

The kids headed back to the train. On their way through the hallway at the back of the arena, they passed the guard who had chased them earlier. He was sound asleep, leaning against the wall where he had stopped to catch his breath. The Little Wanderers felt bad about having run away so Kaya fetched a cup of water and put it next to him. “Now he’ll have a refreshing drink when he wakes up,” she explained.

The children slipped back through the fence and onto the train. AJ set the dial to return home and pulled back on the gearshift. In a flash, they were back in Papa Lemon’s shed.

Everyone was excited to tell Papa Lemon and Mama Sarah about the Olympics and about meeting Babe again. “Don’t be afraid to revisit an adventure. You never know what you will see the second time,” Papa Lemon said.

Nikki was still smiling from ear to ear. “Yes, the second trip was perfect. Now we can write a great paper about Babe Didrikson,” she said, and they all headed to the attic to do just that.

Meet the Author, Lehman Riley

When I was in 3rd grade, I used to daydream about summer trips to my grandparents' house. My grandfather, Papa Lemon, fascinated me; in my eyes, he was a celebrity. I wrote my daydreams about him into this book.

I now reside in Minneapolis, Minnesota with my wife Tracy and my four children, DuVale, Nareece, Andrea and Tianna.

Meet the Illustrator, Joshua Wallace

My interest in drawing started when I could pick up a crayon and scribble. Childrens books were my first big inspiration. They taught me to never neglect the depths of imagination and to never forget how to think like a child.

I currently work as an illustrator and graphic designer and live in Blaine, Minnesota.

Other Papa Lemon Adventures:

Book 1: Meeting Dr. Martin Luther King
Book 2: The Dangerous Escape from Slavery
Book 3: World War II, The Navajo Wind Talkers
Book 4: The Life of Babe Didrikson "Greatness is Never Forgotten"